D1508529

HUNGER GAMES

TRIBUTE GUIDE

by Emily Seife

Scholastic Press • New York

ACKNOWLEDGMENTS
Thank you to Yon Elvira, Amanda Maes, and Douglas Lloyd at Lionsgate,
and to David Levithan, Rick DeMonico, Paul Banks, Erin Black, and Lindsay Walter at Scholastic.
And with much gratitude to Suzanne Collins.
— E.S.

Library of Congress Cataloging-in-Publication Data available
ISBN 978-0-545-45782-8

10 9 8 7 6 5 4 3   12 13 14 15 16 17/0
Printed in the U.S.A.   23
First edition, March 2012

This book was designed by Rick DeMonico

CONTENTS

CITIZENS OF PANEM,
ARE YOU READY?
YOU'VE BEEN WAITING
ALL YEAR, AND THE
TIME HAS FINALLY COME
ONCE AGAIN....

FOLLOW THE CAMERAS AS
THEY SWOOP OUT OF THE
GLITTERING STREETS OF
THE CAPITOL, SPEED
DOWN THE TRAIN TRACKS
THAT CRISSCROSS OUR
GREAT NATION, AND
TAKE YOU OUT TO THE
FARTHEST REACHES OF
THE DISTRICTS.

Welcome to Panem's Seventy-fourth Hunger Games.

INTRODUCTION

INTRODUCTION

There was once a place called North America. But droughts and fires, hurricanes and tornados, and encroaching seas took their toll. Brutal wars broke out as people fought for the few remaining resources. The earth was scarred and desolate, the people terrified and hopeless.

But out of the ashes and the wreckage rose Panem, a nation made up of a great Capitol ringed by thirteen districts, which brought peace and prosperity to its citizens for many generations.

Then came the Dark Days, the uprising of the districts against the Capitol. The shining light of our nation was clouded by war — terrible war. The thirteen districts rebelled against the country that fed them, loved them, and protected them. Their revolt left the country in tatters. Motherless children filled the streets. The land was torn asunder. After a long struggle, in which many died, there came a hard-won peace. Twelve districts were defeated, the thirteenth obliterated. When the traitors were at last suppressed, we swore as a nation we would never allow such treason again.

Thus was the Treaty of Treason written and signed, providing us with new laws to live by — laws that would guarantee peace. As a yearly reminder that the Dark Days must never come again, it was decreed on the same day each year, the various districts would offer up in tribute one brave young man and one brave young woman to fight in a pageant of honor, courage, and sacrifice — the Hunger Games. The twenty-four tributes are sent to an outdoor arena, where they struggle to overcome both man and nature, and triumph over the odds. Each year, the lone victor serves as a reminder of the nation's generosity and forgiveness.

This season is both a time for repentance and a time for thanks. This is how we remember our past. This is how we safeguard our future.

Now the great nation of Panem, ruled by the shining Capitol, consists of twelve districts, each essential in its own way. Each district concentrates on producing one resource, so that only together do the districts form a cohesive, powerful whole. The Capitol collects and redistributes the food and the fuel so that every district, and every family, has what it needs to prosper.

DISTRICT 1: LUXURY

District 1 makes the luxury goods that decorate and beautify our great Capitol. Its excellent taste and craftsmanship keep Capitol residents bewigged and bedazzled year-round.

DISTRICT 2: MASONRY

Our nation would be nothing without District 2's superb stonework. It builds and fortifies our cities, and its citizens are known individually for their strength.

DISTRICT 3: TECHNOLOGY

Panem is one of the most advanced nations in mankind's history, thanks to the efforts of District 3. Its computers keep us all connected, and its electronic gadgets keep us all entertained.

DISTRICT 4: FISHING

Do you like seafood? Shrimp and crabmeat? Often overlooked, District 4 plays an essential role, bringing us the bounty of the sea. These citizens are adept with nets and tridents, and can swim like fish themselves.

DISTRICT 5: POWER

Electric, solar, and nuclear — District 5 harnesses the energy of the earth and the sky in order to power our great nation.

DISTRICT 6: TRANSPORTATION

Our hovercraft, our high-speed trains, and our cargo trains come to us from District 6. Ironically, the citizens here have little love for travel.

DISTRICT 7: LUMBER

This beautiful district is lush with trees, from which these citizens supply our lumber and paper. The people of District 7 are hardworking and down-to-earth.

DISTRICT 8: TEXTILES

From the simple, lovely fabrics of the districts to the beautiful brocades favored in the Capitol, District 8 makes it all.

DISTRICT 9: GRAIN

District 9 is Panem's bread bowl, giving us the fertile harvest we need to keep rising as a nation. Its amber waves of grain are an inspiration to us all.

DISTRICT 10: LIVESTOCK

The gentle lowing of cattle is the first thing a visitor to District 10 hears. This region raises strong, healthy livestock, which becomes the meat that helps us raise strong, healthy children of Panem.

DISTRICT 11: AGRICULTURE

Known for its bountiful orchards, District 11's workers spend their days among rustling fruit trees and sizable farms.

DISTRICT 12: MINING

One of the outer districts, this is nonetheless a crucial one. These brave and hardy workers descend deep into the earth each day to mine the coal that keeps our nation running.

THE REAPING

THE HUNGER GAMES SEASON ALWAYS BEGINS WITH THE REAPINGS.

On the reaping day, citizens in all the districts across Panem gather in their town squares. In each district, two names are selected from two large glass globes — the names of the new male and female tributes. In front of the Hall of Justice and the seal of Panem, the people of the districts wait to hear who will represent them in the Games.

All citizens in all twelve districts from the ages of twelve to eighteen are entered into the selection pool for the Hunger Games. At age twelve, your name is entered once. At thirteen, twice. By the age of eighteen, the final year of eligibility, your name goes into the pool seven times.

A citizen can also choose to receive a tessera — a year's supply of grain and oil — in return for adding his or her name an additional time to the pool. One can choose to do this for family members, too. Many people take the gamble, opting for the extra rations and facing the increased risk.

Upon arrival, each citizen of eligible age must register with a worker from the Capitol. The worker wears rubber gloves in order to perform the job safely. One by one, this worker takes each citizen's finger, quickly pricks it, and blots the blood into a ledger. Then a small scanner is passed over the blood, registering the person's information. "EVERDEEN, KATNISS. 16/YO."

"EVERDEEN, PRIMROSE. 12/YO." This way, the Capitol can keep track of who is newly eligible, who has taken tesserae, and who has grown too old for the Games.

In District 12, the reaping takes place in the town square, where a temporary stage holds a microphone and chairs for local officials and the district's only living victor. The town square is a good meeting place for most of the year, but on reaping day, it can be a bit crowded and imposing. The citizens of the districts are all decked out in their finest outfits for the reaping. They're eager, but also silent and respectful as the ceremony is about to begin. The twelve- through eighteen-year-olds stand in a cordoned-off area, grouped by age, with the oldest in the front. Adults must stay behind the ropes, as they are there purely as spectators.

Peacekeepers line the squares. They stand at attention, making sure the day proceeds smoothly and according to plan.

There is a festive feeling in the air. The districts eagerly anticipate competing against one another for the victor's crown. And while the folks back home will root for their tributes, they will also be thinking of the benefits they will receive if one of their own emerges victorious: The winner's district is showered with extra food rations — grain, oil, and sugar in abundance.

Once everyone is registered and in place, the district's escort starts the ceremony. Effie Trinket is the lovely escort for District 12. With a new wig for every occasion, Effie knows how to keep things fresh and fun. She spends the majority of her year home in the Capitol, but comes out to the district in order to help shepherd the new tributes through the sometimes overwhelming process of preparing for the Games. She also acts as announcer for District 12's reaping.

"Happy Hunger Games!" she says. "And may the odds be ever in your favor!"

She graciously thanks everyone, smiling and saying what a huge honor it is for her to be here. After showing a film that reviews the history of the Hunger Games — how it began seventy-four years ago, after the Capitol put down the rebellion, and how the Games serve as a reminder to the districts never to rebel again — Effie is ready to pick the names.

"Ladies first!" she says.

She reaches her pale, elegant arm deep into a large glass ball, and rummages around. This action is performed twenty-four times over the course of the day, and each time there is total silence across Panem.

Who will it be this year? The nation holds its breath.

Effie removes her hand. "Primrose Everdeen."

A slight, blonde twelve-year-old begins to walk forward to accept the honor. But before she can get very far, a voice rings out above the crowd. "Prim!" Dashing forward is a dark-haired girl in a plain blue dress. "I volunteer!" she calls. "I volunteer as tribute!"

This replacement is an especially gripping turn of events because, while volunteers are a common occurrence in Districts 1 and 2, we rarely see them step up in the other districts. A murmur of surprise runs through the crowd as they react to this sudden change of fortunes.

"Ladies and gentleman, what an *exciting* moment!" Effie Trinket exclaims.

As the young woman steps onto the stage, Effie asks the audience for a big round of applause, then introduces this newcomer to Panem. And so

Katniss Everdeen becomes the female tribute from District 12. On the reaping day, Katniss doesn't seem too chatty. But the audience knows she'll open up for her big interview in the Capitol!

Meanwhile, a handsome, dark-haired young man has to carry little Primrose away from her sister. Viewers around the nation are spellbound by the family drama playing out on the big screen. The young man

disappears into the crowd. Sources will not confirm whether he is a friend or a family member.

In the back of the crowd, behind the roped-off area, Katniss's mother watches silently from the crowd. She also declines to comment.

But now it's time to choose the male tribute! Effie reaches into another glass ball and snatches a paper slip from the very top.

"Peeta Mellark!"

The new tribute makes his way to the stage. He is of medium height and stocky build, with dirty blond hair that lies in smooth waves. He remains composed as he walks forward.

Though this year's District 12 male tribute, Peeta Mellark, is initially overshadowed by Katniss's act of generosity, he's still someone to look out for in the arena.

The reaping is complete, and Katniss and Peeta now take their places among the twenty-four tributes of the Seventy-fourth Hunger Games!

THE TRIBUTES

GLIMMER

GENDER: FEMALE

HEIGHT: 5'7"

LUXURY

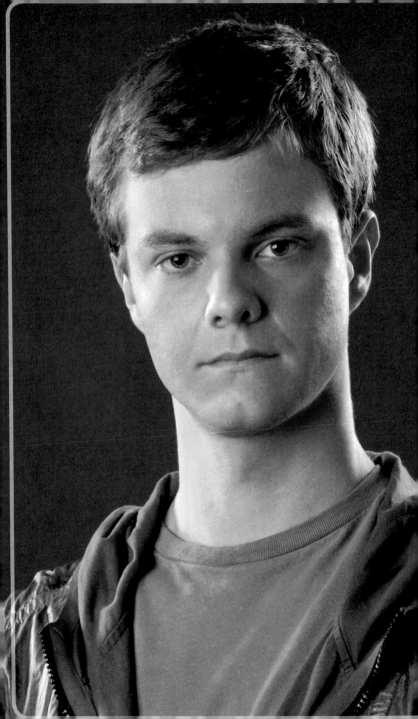

MARVEL
GENDER: MALE
HEIGHT: 6'3"
WEAPON: SPEAR

LUXURY

CLOVE

GENDER: FEMALE

HEIGHT: 5'4"

WEAPON: THROWING KNIVES

MASONRY

DISTRICT

·2·

CATO

GENDER: MALE

AGE: 16

HEIGHT: 6′2″

WEAPON: SWORD, MACHETE

MASONRY

TRIBUTE GIRL

GENDER: FEMALE

HEIGHT: 5'9"

TECHNOLOGY

TRIBUTE BOY

GENDER: MALE

HEIGHT: 4'8"

WEAPON: MINES

TECHNOLOGY

DISTRICT

·4·

TRIBUTE GIRL
GENDER: FEMALE
HEIGHT: 5'4"

FISHING

TRIBUTE BOY
GENDER: MALE

HEIGHT: 4'8"

FISHING

FOXFACE

GENDER: FEMALE

HEIGHT: 5′5″

WEAPON: STEALTH

POWER

DISTRICT

·5·

TRIBUTE BOY

GENDER: MALE

HEIGHT: 5'7"

POWER

DISTRICT

·6·

TRIBUTE GIRL

GENDER: FEMALE

HEIGHT: 4´11˝

TRANSPORTATION

DISTRICT

·6·

TRIBUTE BOY

GENDER: MALE

HEIGHT: 5'10"

TRANSPORTATION

TRIBUTE GIRL

GENDER: FEMALE

AGE: 16

HEIGHT: 4'11"

LUMBER

DISTRICT · 7

TRIBUTE BOY
GENDER: MALE
AGE: 16
HEIGHT: 5′3″

LUMBER

DISTRICT

·8·

TRIBUTE GIRL

GENDER: FEMALE

HEIGHT: 5'7"

TEXTILES

TRIBUTE BOY

GENDER: MALE

HEIGHT: 6'

TEXTILES

DISTRICT ·9·

TRIBUTE GIRL

GENDER: FEMALE

HEIGHT: 5'1"

GRAIN

TRIBUTE BOY

GENDER: MALE

HEIGHT: 4'11"

GRAIN

DISTRICT · 10

TRIBUTE GIRL
GENDER: FEMALE
HEIGHT: 5'4"

LIVESTOCK

DISTRICT · 10

TRIBUTE BOY

GENDER: MALE

HEIGHT: 5'8"

LIVESTOCK

RUE

GENDER: FEMALE

AGE: 12

HEIGHT: 4'8"

WEAPON: SLINGSHOT

AGRICULTURE

DISTRICT · 11

THRESH

GENDER: MALE

HEIGHT: 6'

WEAPON: ROCK

AGRICULTURE

KATNISS

GENDER: FEMALE

AGE: 16

HEIGHT: 5'7"

WEAPON: BOW AND ARROW

MINING

PEETA

GENDER: MALE

AGE: 16

HEIGHT: 5'10"

WEAPON: SPEAR, CAMOUFLAGE, STRENGTH

MINING

THE TRAIN

The next step in the journey of the tributes is to board the luxury train that whisks them from their home districts to the Capitol. Many tributes have never left their home districts, so this sudden adventure is always exciting. The Capitol trains are very different from the coal trains a district citizen might be used to. These trains can average 250 miles per hour.

The interior of the train is just as impressive. Tributes get their own chambers, which include a bedroom, dressing room, and private bathroom. They get to enjoy the best of the Capitol as they speed across the country: gorgeous floral arrangements, delectable foods, and lush surroundings. Beverages of every flavor and every color. Crystal chandeliers, china teacups, and silver candelabra. It's all very new to the tributes from the outer districts. They're not accustomed to the bounty of the Capitol. Tributes have been known to stuff themselves with the rich Capitol food and arrive at the Training Center with a stomachache.

As they travel, the tributes can peer out the windows at the countryside flying by. They might get a brief glimpse of another district — or of the ruins of a fallen city from long-ago North America. Tributes often say that this high-speed tour of the country is one of the highlights of the time leading up to the Hunger Games.

"UNFORTUNATELY, I CAN'T SEAL THE SPONSOR DEALS FOR YOU. ONLY HAYMITCH CAN DO THAT."
— EFFIE TRINKET

On the train, the tributes have a chance to sit down for a long chat with their new mentors. All mentors are winners of previous Hunger Games. Haymitch Abernathy is the District 12 mentor, and currently the only living victor from that district. At the age of sixteen, Haymitch became victor of the Fiftieth Hunger

Games — a Quarter Quell — which had four tributes from each district, rather than two. It was an unusually challenging year, making Haymitch's victory all the more impressive.

A seasoned veteran of the game and an experienced mentor, Haymitch is also known for liking liquor a bit too much. He's often a source of entertainment when he arrives in the Capitol each year. However, he's not known for getting sponsors for his protégés. Let's hope he gets his act together and gives Katniss and Peeta some good advice this year!

Effie is also on the train — and has brought plenty of wild outfits with her. Effie instructs the tributes on how they can best ingratiate themselves in the Capitol environment. Believe it or not, some tributes have to be told not to eat with their fingers! Not these two, though. It's clear Katniss and Peeta have both been raised well. This will help them as they head to the Remake Center.

THE
REMAKE CENTER

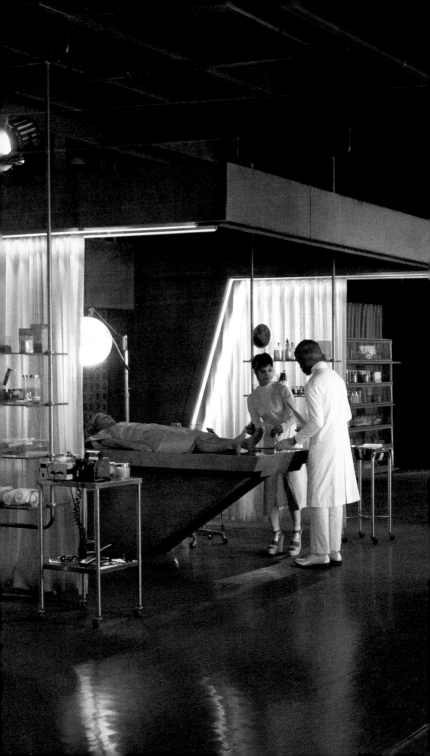

When the tributes arrive in the Capitol, they're immediately taken to the Remake Center. Standards of care are not as high in the districts, where people bathe less frequently and barely give a thought to how they present themselves.

In the Remake Center, the prep teams scrub the dirt and grime of the outer districts away. The tributes enjoy letting the stress of their travels fall away under the soothing hands of the prep teams. The prep teams burnish the tributes' skin with exfoliating foam, untangle and brush out their hair, give them manicures and pedicures, and remove body hair with warm wax when necessary. In the end, the tributes emerge sparkling clean, with smooth, glowing skin, ready for the stylists to work their magic!

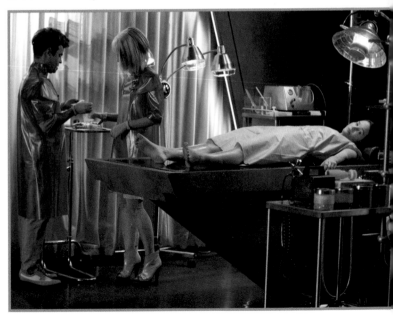

All the prep teams have been training their whole lives. Working on the look of the tributes is a great honor. Katniss's prep team consists of Venia, Flavius, and Octavia. They're completely fashionable, and can do wonders with a little makeup.

Next, tributes meet with their stylists. Cinna is the stylist for the District 12 female, Katniss, and is known in the Capitol as a bit of a renegade — a real artist. A handsome man in his late thirties, Cinna doesn't

follow the fickle fashions of the Capitol or try to impress with elaborate wigs. He's always simply dressed in plain black clothes, perhaps with an elegant necklace and just a touch of sparkling eye makeup.

Portia is the stylist for the District 12 male, Peeta. Together, she and Cinna make the perfect team.

What will Cinna and Portia come up with for tributes Katniss and Peeta? Traditionally, District 12 tributes have appeared in the tribute parade as some interpretation of coal miners. One year, the tributes emerged stark naked and covered in coal dust. We'll have to wait and see what the stylists create this year!

Who are the main forces behind this year's Hunger Games
Let's introduce them. . . .

President Snow, our noble leader, has helped our country become
prosperous and secure. He watches over all the districts and metes out
justice with a firm hand. He traditionally makes a short speech welcoming th
tributes during the opening ceremonies, but leaves most of the running of th
Games to the Head Gamemaker, and to the announcer, Claudius Templesmit

Still, just because you don't see President Snow, it doesn't mean he's not
watching every minute of the action. To our president, the Games are the
heart of Panem.

rane is the Head Gamemaker of the Seventy-fourth Hunger
summate showman and a true entertainer, Seneca is sure to
of the most breathtaking, edge-of-your-seat Hunger Games
known in fashion circles for his unique beard.

it really mean to be Head Gamemaker? Seneca Crane's
s include supervising the construction of the arena, making
ing ceremonies run smoothly, assessing the talents of the
es, and adjusting the features of the arena to fit their strengths
ses. Once the Games begin, the Gamemakers retreat to their
, which is a virtual center where they control all aspects of the
s: the weather, the environment, and the action.

TRIBUTE PARADE

TRIBUTE PARADE

Once their prep teams and stylists have put on the finishing touches, the opening ceremonies are ready to begin!

One by one, each pair rides a horse-drawn chariot down the Avenue of the Tributes, past President Snow and other government officials. The streets are packed with people, and the crowds go wild when they see the first tributes emerge. The costumes are spectacular!

First out are Glimmer and Marvel from District 1. Their district's specialty is luxury goods — and doesn't that show in their fabulous getups! Tall, regal Glimmer looks magnificent with a pink feather headdress and a full-length gown. Note the feathery shoulder treatment. Exquisite! Next to her, Marvel is looking *marvelous* in black leather boots and a fuchsia cape. We think these two will be a force to be reckoned with in the upcoming Games!

Wow! Next out are Clove and Cato from District 2, and they are truly stunning. In traditional-style garb, like ancient Greek gods, the two look positively divine. Clove's golden helmet emphasizes her beautiful bone structure. We can't help but wonder if her stylists are trying to foreshadow another golden crown —

the victor's crown, which would look spectacular on Clove's dark hair. Cato's sleeveless costume shows off his arms to good effect — wouldn't want to wrestle with him in the arena! These two look like the serious contenders that they are.

From the technology district, District 3, emerge two tributes in silver mesh. They wear sculpted silver head-dresses that resemble the intricate inner workings of electronics.

"I JUST LOVE HOW CLEVER THE STYLISTS ARE EVERY YEAR, REFLECTING THE CHARACTER OF EACH DISTRICT."
— CAESAR FLICKERMAN

Next comes another beautifully dressed duo. With starfish pins on their shoulders and luminous pearls in their hair, it is clearly the chariot from District 4, our fishing district. This male tribute is a young one. He looks to be straight from his first reaping; can't be more than twelve years old there.

From District 5 we have two young contestants in glittering silver from head to toe — it's clear they are power-plant workers. Their costumes reflect and refract the light every time they move. Very striking! But the female tribute from this district has something a little sly in her eyes. Don't turn your back on her in the arena!

District 6, transportation, always keeps our country moving. Let's wish those two tributes the best of luck as they go by.

The folded fan headdresses, the carefully curled and pleated sleeves . . . In all white, clean and pure as a new sheet of paper, our tributes from lumber and paper-producing District 7! We wonder what stories will be written on these blank slates.

Now please turn your attention — and your applause — to the next chariot. The tributes wear serious expressions, framed by such playful costumes! With a variety of colors, textures, and materials in their outfits, they must be the tributes from District 8, textiles!

The District 9 tributes look elegant and determined. We love the gold and silver outfits they're wearing. Could the decorative rows on his costume symbolize rows of grain? Or are their stylists simply using those reflective materials to catch the audience's attention?

From District 10, livestock, we have a modern take on the classic cowboy outfit — hats and plaid and all. Gold is a popular color this year! Take note, Capitol fashionistas.

BEHIND THE SCENES WITH STYLIST CINNA!

"Portia and I think that coal miner thing's very overdone. No one will remember you in that. And we both see it as our job to make the District Twelve tributes unforgettable," says Cinna. . . . "So rather than focus on the coal mining itself, we're going to focus on the coal. . . . And what do we do with coal? We burn it."

And nearing the end, District 11 is a study in contrasts! The female tribute, Rue, looks to be just twelve years old, and well under five feet; the male tribute, Thresh, must be at least six feet tall and solid muscle! The two do make a nice pair, though, in their agriculture-themed overalls and leafy crowns.

But what's that back there? Ladies and gentleman, there's something brand-new and exciting this year — the tributes from District 12 are . . . on fire!

Katniss Everdeen and Peeta Mellark stand tall and proud, hand in hand, trailing fire as their chariot moves down the avenue. Two coal-black horses lead them forward. Flames flicker off their bodies and reflect in their sparkling eyes. When Katniss picks up a rose, she wins a lot of hearts — and maybe even some sponsors. Katniss Everdeen captured the nation's attention when she volunteered to take her sister's place, and she's certainly doing a good job of keeping it. Though they've been on a long losing streak, District 12 might just have a fighting chance in this year's Games.

Once all the tributes have reached the street, attention turns to President Snow. He stands at the podium at the head of the avenue and delivers his address.

"Welcome."

His voice is greeted with enormous cheers from the masses in attendance.

"Tributes! We welcome you. We salute your courage and your sacrifice and we wish you all . . . Happy Hunger Games! And may the odds be ever in your favor."

The crowd roars in appreciation. They are standing now, stomping and clapping — and as the sound swells to a fever pitch, the tributes disappear into the Training Center. The doors shut behind them with a resounding clang.

Now the people of the Capitol will have some time to mull over what they've seen. Who looked strong, and who looked clever? Whose entrance seemed a little dull — and whose was fiery? The next the audience will see of the tributes will be the interviews with Caesar Flickerman. But before that, we're pleased to be able to take you on an exclusive backstage tour of the Training Center, where we'll show you what the tributes themselves are experiencing.

BEHIND THE SCENES WITH STYLIST CINNA!

After the procession, everyone was buzzing about the Girl on Fire. How was it that the two tributes, Katniss and Peeta, were in flames, but never burned? Cinna divulges that he and partner, Portia, dressed the tributes in black leather from neck to ankle, and used a synthetic fire to create the striking effect. He tells us that he used very little makeup on the two (naturally attractive) tributes, just adding a little highlighting here and there.

THE TRAINING
CENTER

Here's the heart of the complex — the Training Center itself. We're happy to offer our readers an exclusive look at the stations of the Training Center and the weapons the tributes train with.

The Training Center is a massive, open gym. Bright lights illuminate the area from above. The cavernous space echoes with the sound of grunts and clashing weapons. In the corner, a few tributes engage in hand-to-hand combat with a trainer in body armor. They roar as they hurtle their bodies toward each other. In another corner there's the flash of metal, as blades fly through the air. Knives stab . . . spears are hurled . . . an ax lodges itself in a soft target. A closer look reveals that the targets are life-sized human shapes.

The Careers, the tributes from Districts 1 and 2, are eager to show off. They project an aura of arrogance in order to intimidate their competition. Once in the gym, they head straight for the sharpest weapons.

To keep everyone safe, Peacekeepers with stun guns are placed around the room. They stay out of the training, but are quick to step in if a fight breaks out.

In a special area, perched above the gym, is the Gamemakers' balcony. From the balcony, the Gamemakers have a clear view of all the tributes in the room. Sometimes they take notes, sometimes they help themselves to a lavish buffet, but they are always paying close attention to the action below them. They are studying the tributes: how they move, how they interact, how they jump, and how they fall. All this knowledge will come into play once the Games begin.

Meet Atala, the head trainer. She can whip even the weakest tribute into shape. When they first enter the Center, she gathers them in a circle in the center of the space so that she can explain the rules. "No fighting with other tributes," she says. "You'll have plenty of time for that in the arena." Atala starts to point out the various training stations. "My advice is DON'T IGNORE the survival skills. Twenty-three of you will die. One will not. Who that is depends on your ability to anticipate. Everyone wants to grab a sword but lots of you will die of natural causes. Ten percent from infection. Twenty percent from dehydration. One year the arena was a frozen tundra. Five years ago it was a burning desert. Exposure can kill you as easily as a knife."

She blows her whistle. The training has begun.

‘MAKE SURE THEY REMEMBER YOU.’’
— HAYMITCH ABERNATHY

THE GAUNTLET

The gauntlet is a daunting obstacle course. It consists of ascending platforms that rise up to a landing. The tributes must jump from platform to platform to reach the finish in the fastest time possible. To make it even more challenging, they must do it while trainers swing at them with padded clubs. What skills will help with the gauntlet? Speed, of course. Agility. You want to be able to duck and dodge your way around those swinging clubs. But strength and balance help, too. If you do get hit, can you keep yourself steady?

ROPES COURSE

A large net stretches to the ceiling of the gym. Again, a test of many things, including strength and balance and agility. Be warned: This climbing net is harder than it looks.

Ropes stretch across the ceiling, too. But only the very nimble can leap around up there.

Could you pull yourself up a hanging rope using sheer muscle? We suspect this tribute can.

SNARES

If you're in the arena, you want to be able to catch your own food. You could gather it . . . shoot it . . . fish for it . . . or catch it with a snare. Katniss Everdeen seems quite at home in this station. It's hard to see through the tall grass, but it looks like she's figured out an intricate rope snare.

CAMOUFLAGE

You may think this station looks more "arts and crafts" than arena, but there is some benefit to knowing how to camouflage yourself. Look here at Peeta's arm pressed up against the tree trunk. The arm is painted with a bark pattern, with light green moss.

WEIGHTS

Here you can find regular weights . . . and also iron balls with studs and spikes. Can you throw one like a shot put? Can you even pick one up?

H

ere's a close look at some of the weapons favored by the tributes in the Training Center gym.

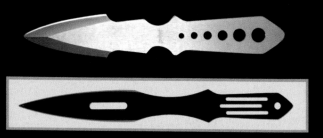

CLOVE'S TRAINING CENTER KNIVES

PEETA'S TRAINING CENTER MEDICINE BALL

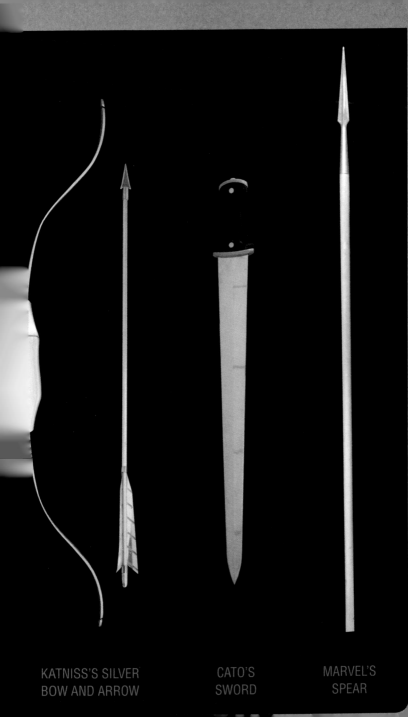

KATNISS'S SILVER
BOW AND ARROW

CATO'S
SWORD

MARVEL'S
SPEAR

Let's follow the tributes into their quarters in the Training Center for a special glimpse into their lives before the Games.

Sometimes the tributes just need to grab some private time together. Maybe they're discussing strategy. Or maybe they're relaxing, taking a break from the lights and cameras and ardent fans that constantly follow them.

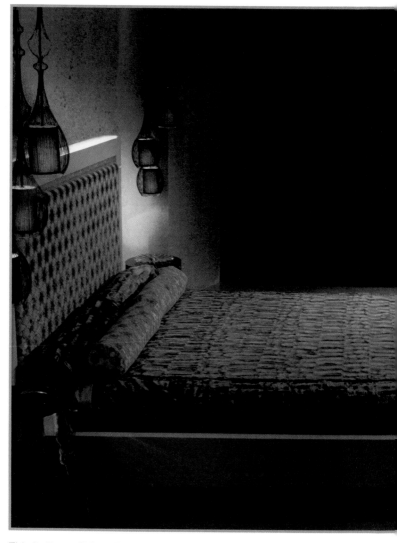

This is the stylish and modern bedroom of the
District 12 female tribute, Katniss Everdeen. All the
conveniences of the Capitol are provided here:

high-tech shower, full-body blow-drying when you are
done bathing, and a closet full of outfits designed to fit
any taste.

The tributes usually dine with their mentors and stylists.
Here, Katniss is joined by Effie Trinket, Cinna, and Portia.
The Capitol treats them to all-you-can-eat banquets with
the finest food Panem has to offer. Exotic sushi, mashed

potatoes, wine, puffy bread, slices of pale purple melon, cheese and sweet blue grapes, hot chocolate . . . waited on hand and foot by Avox servers, the tributes live the high life in the days leading up to the Games.

INDIVIDUAL SESSIONS

"THE EVALUATIONS ARE IMPORTANT BECAUSE A HIGHER RATING WILL MEAN SPONSORS."
— HAYMITCH ABERNATHY

The Gamemakers usually get a good sense of the tributes from the general training, but the most important part of training comes at the very end: the private sessions. Each tribute has a brief period alone

in the gym to show the Gamemakers what they can do. Sometimes a good strategy is to intimidate the other players during training. But sometimes a clever strategy is to keep your talent hidden from the other tributes until you reach the arena, so you can take them by surprise. The private session is the perfect time to show the Gamemakers if you have any skills you've been keeping secret so far. Based on your session and your performance over the past few days, the Gamemakers will give a score from one to twelve. A higher score means they think you have a better chance of winning the Hunger Games.

Tributes sit on a long bench in the waiting area until they are called. Atala is there to usher them in. Katniss and Peeta from District 12 are the last two to be summoned. Their footsteps echo in the long hallway. Let's hope they're not too nervous to do a good job.

What happens in these private sessions is confidential, known to no one but the tribute and the Gamemakers. The rest of us have to wait for the scores to come out. Even then, we can only guess at what the tributes did to earn their rankings.

After all the private sessions with the Gamemakers have been conducted, the tributes return to their separate quarters and grab a quick dinner. Then they assemble in the viewing rooms to watch the results come in. Here, the District 12 team — Cinna, Effie, Haymitch, Katniss, Peeta, and Portia — gathers in their viewing room. As ever, an Avox waits in the background, ready to serve, but the team's attention is fixed on the television. You can see in their postures how tense of a moment this is for them, as their scores are announced live to the nation.

"The tributes were rated on a scale of one to twelve, after three days of careful evaluation," Caesar Flickerman announces. "The Gamekeepers want to acknowledge that it was an exceptional group of tributes, as the scores in a moment will indicate."

One by one, the scores trickle in. The Careers get scores in the eight-to-ten range. Very respectable, but hardly a shock. The other players' scores vary, but most are around a five. One surprise in the bunch is Rue, the tiny little tribute from District 11, who somehow manages to get a seven.

Last to be announced are the District 12 scores.

Caesar Flickerman: "And finally from District Twelve. Peeta Mellark. A score of eight."

The group exchanges words of relief and encouragement. This is a solid score that could help Peeta in the arena. Cinna claps briefly, but Caesar's still talking. . . .

"And our last tribute . . . Katniss Everdeen: a score of . . ."

At this point, Caesar Flickerman pauses and double-checks his sheet. Did he read it right? Is this an error?

". . . eleven."

INTERVIEWS

INTERVIEWS

"Okay, ladies and gentlemen. This is it."

— Caesar Flickerman

Our host for the evening, as always, is the inimitable Caesar Flickerman. With his trademark colored hair and sparkling suit, Caesar is skilled at coaxing shy tributes out of their shells. He really knows how to work an audience.

Now, Caesar opens up the Hunger Games pregame gala with a broad smile. Bright spotlights shine onstage. His jacket — and the whole stage in fact — glitters in the light. Soon, all of the tributes will come out onstage for interviews with Caesar. This is the moment when the tributes will open up to the audience. They've had a chance to win sponsors with their looks and their physical skills, but here's a chance for them to show how smart or personable or funny they are. Maybe they share a little story from back home. Maybe they give Caesar a hint of what their strategy

will be in the Games. Maybe they just smile and flirt. We'll see what reveals we have this year. . . .

Katniss Everdeen has been all the buzz in the Capitol. She's even known as the Girl on Fire since making such a bright showing at the tribute parade. The audience is eager to hear what she has to say for herself. But there's a long roster of interviews before the District 12 tributes will take the hot seat.

The tributes get dolled up in a backstage dressing room, then line up in anticipation of their interviews. You really remember how young they are when you see how impatient they get waiting!

As always, the interviews start with the lowest numbered district. First on the list is Glimmer. The beautiful blonde bombshell from District 1 looks pretty thrilled to be here. A Career, Glimmer has been training for the Games her whole life. Caesar compliments her outfit, and the crowd goes wild. Glimmer clearly knows how to work the crowd.

Other highlights from the interviews include Marvel, the male tribute from District 1, who has a happy, positive presence onstage, but doesn't seem to be the sharpest tool in the shed. Cato, the male tribute from District 2, wins over the audience with his charming,

slightly cocky persona. Clove, from District 2, looks absolutely stunning in a frilly, orange dress with ribbon trim, and her hair piled in elegant twists atop her head. A bit of sarcasm mixed in with the sweetness keeps her interview interesting. The fox-faced girl from District 5 comes across as sly and elusive. Another highlight from the interviews is little Rue from District 11. This lovely twelve-year-old has captivated the audience. But does she have a chance in the arena?

Finally, the Girl on Fire makes her appearance onstage. She's in a gorgeous, fire-red, off-the-shoulder gown.

"That was quite an entrance you made at the tribute parade. Can you tell us about it?" Caesar asks.

"Oh, well . . . I just hoped I wouldn't get burned to death."

Mild laughter greets Katniss's statement, and it's clear that the nervous tribute starts to relax. As Caesar and Katniss continue to chat, she warms up to the audience even more. Finally, Katniss surprises and delights the audience when she stands up and twirls. In motion, her dress reveals itself to be flickering and bright — she's still on fire, all right!

Katniss ends her interview by declaring that she will be trying to win the Hunger Games — for her little sister, Prim. A huge ovation greets her touching statement.

But it's Peeta who throws the real shocker this evening. He's funny and warm onstage, immediately likeable. He jokes back and forth with Caesar, keeping him on his toes with sharp repartee. Caesar asks Peeta if he has a girl back home — a special someone.

"There is one girl I've had a crush on for-ever — but I don't think she even noticed me till the reaping."

"Well, I tell you what you do. You go out there and you *win* this thing and when you get home, she'll have to go out with you."

"I don't think that's going to help. Winning won't mat-ter in my case."

"Why not?" Caesar asks.

"Because — she came here with me."

JOURNEY TO THE ARENA

> **"THEY'LL PUT ALL SORTS OF STUFF RIGHT IN FRONT. RIGHT IN THE MOUTH OF THE CORNUCOPIA. THERE WILL EVEN BE A BOW. BUT DON'T GO FOR IT. . . . THEY'RE TRYING TO PULL YOU IN AND IT'S NOT YOUR GAME. TURN. RUN. GET TO HIGH GROUND AND THEN FIND SOME WATER."**
>
> — HAYMITCH ABERNATHY

Mentors give their tributes a last few pieces of advice before they are taken to the arena. Then the tributes step into a hovercraft, to be flown to a staging ground beneath the arena.

They sit in two long rows of seats. Peacekeepers watch over them, strong and silent. The tributes are all very aware of one another, of where they are going, but no one makes eye contact. A woman in a white lab coat goes down the row, inserting a tracker into each tribute's arm so the Gamemakers can follow every-one's vital statistics and positions in the arena. She pushes a thin syringe into their arms, and the small device is in place.

The windows of the hovercraft darken as the vehicle approaches the arena, so that the location will be obscured. It pulls into an underground bunker. Each tribute is escorted by Peacekeepers down a long hall and into their private Launch Room, marked with their ID: "FEMALE 12."

LAUNCH ROOM

The Launch Rooms are located directly underneath the arena — below the Cornucopia. They are brand-new. The arenas are used only once, then designated as historic sites. Preserved, they become popular vacation destinations for Capitol travelers. So this is the only time these rooms will be used by tributes.

In the Launch Rooms, the tributes receive their clothes for the Games. The outfits are the same for all the tributes, but each district has a distinct color to distinguish them in the arena.

Each tribute has a moment alone with his or her stylist in the Launch Room before being brought up to the surface. They may exchange a few private words, a few last pieces of encouragement.

Once ready, the tributes go stand in the cylindrical tubes that will bring them up to the arena. The twenty-four cylinders begin to rise. For fifteen seconds, the tributes stand in utter darkness, hearts pounding. Then the metal plate pushes them out into the open air, to whatever future awaits.

"LADIES AND GENTLEMEN, LET THE SEVENTY-FOURTH HUNGER GAMES BEGIN!"